Poppy and Max and the Noisy Night

For Emilia
SG

For Molly May with love x
LG

Reading Consultant: Prue Goodwin,
lecturer in education at the University of Reading

ORCHARD BOOKS
338 Euston Road, London NW1 3BH
Orchard Books Australia
Level 17/207 Kent Street, Sydney, NSW 2000
ISBN: 978 1 84362 407 3 (hardback)
ISBN: 978 1 84362 409 7 (paperback)
First published in hardback in Great Britain in 2007
First paperback publication in 2008
Poppy and Max characters © Lindsey Gardiner 2001
Text © Sally Grindley 2007
Illustrations © Lindsey Gardiner 2007

1 3 5 7 9 10 8 6 4 2 (hardback)
1 3 5 7 9 10 8 6 4 2 (paperback)
Printed in China

Orchard Books is a division of Hachette Children's Books,
an Hachette Livre UK company
www.orchardbooks.co.uk

Poppy and Max and the Noisy Night

Sally Grindley  **Lindsey Gardiner**

ORCHARD BOOKS

One evening Poppy and Max sat by the fire, toasting their toes and playing Snap.

5

"Can you hear the wind, Max?"
asked Poppy. "I love it when the
wind howls down the chimney."

"SNAP!" said Max triumphantly,
and he took the pile of cards.

Poppy giggled. "I'll beat you
next time," she said.

It began to rain.

"Listen to the rain, Max," said Poppy.

"I love it when it pitter-patters on the windows."

"SNAP!" said Max triumphantly,
and he took the pile of cards.
"You're better at this than me,"
giggled Poppy.

Suddenly, a flash of light lit up
the room.
"Brilliant!" cried Poppy. "I love it when
lightning flashes across the sky."

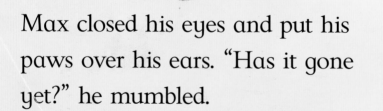

Max closed his eyes and put his
paws over his ears. "Has it gone
yet?" he mumbled.

"SNAP!" cried Poppy happily,
and she took the pile of cards.
"That's not fair," said Max.
"I wasn't watching."
"Never mind, Max," said Poppy.

A rumble of thunder shook the house.
Max leapt onto Poppy's lap. "I don't
like it," he moaned. "Take it away."
"It's all right, Max," said Poppy. "It
won't hurt you."

A great CRASH of thunder
shook the house.
Max howled and burrowed
under the cushions.

"There, there, Max," comforted Poppy.
"I'm not coming out until it's over,"
said Max.

14

The lightning flashed and the thunder
crashed, over and over again.

15

At last, it went quiet.
"You can come out now, Max,"
said Poppy.

"Has it gone?" whimpered Max.
He stuck out his head and listened.

"Time for Snap again," he said.
"Time for bed," said Poppy.

Poppy and Max fell fast asleep. They were woken by a loud BANG!
"Aaaah, what was that?" howled Max.

"It came from downstairs," said Poppy.
"We'd better go and look."
"Do we have to?" said Max.

"Come on Max, I'm sure it's nothing
scary," said Poppy.

They tiptoed downstairs.

In the kitchen they found that a picture
had fallen from the wall.
"I knew there was no need to be
scared," said Max.

They went back to bed and fell
fast asleep.

They were woken by a loud THUMP!
"Aaaah!" yelped Max. "What was that?"

"It came from the bathroom," said
Poppy. "We'll have to go and look."
"Can't you go on your own?" said Max.
"I need you with me," said Poppy.

They tiptoed along the landing.

In the bathroom they found that the soap had fallen into the bath.
"Pah!" said Max. "Nothing to worry about there."

They were just going back to sleep
when they heard a rustling sound.
"It's coming from under the bed!"
said Poppy.
"It's probably mice," said Max.
"I hate mice!" squealed Poppy.

"Mice are all right," said Max.
He dived under the bed, scrabbled
around and popped back up with
a mouse in his paw.

"Take it away, Max, please take
it away," cried Poppy, standing
on the bed.

Max took it downstairs and put it out of the door.
"Thank you, Max," said Poppy.
"You're so brave."

"I am here to protect you," said Max.
"I am a dog and that is what dogs do."
"You're my hero," said Poppy.
"I'm a tired hero," said Max, yawning.

They went back to bed.
"Peace at last," said Poppy, snuggling
down under the covers. But Max was
already fast asleep.

Poppy and **Max**

Sally Grindley
Illustrated by Lindsey Gardiner

Poppy and Max and the Lost Puppy	978 1 84362 392 2	£8.99
Poppy and Max and the Snow Dog	978 1 84362 401 1	£8.99
Poppy and Max and the Fashion Show	978 1 84362 399 1	£8.99
Poppy and Max and the Sore Paw	978 1 84362 402 8	£8.99
Poppy and Max and the River Picnic	978 1 84362 520 9	£8.99
Poppy and Max and the Noisy Night	978 1 84362 407 3	£8.99
Poppy and Max and the Big Wave	978 1 84362 398 4	£8.99
Poppy and Max and Too Many Muffins	978 1 84362 408 0	£8.99

Poppy and Max are available from all good bookshops,
or can be ordered direct from the publisher:
Orchard Books, PO BOX 29, Douglas IM99 1BQ
Credit card orders please telephone 01624 836000 or fax 01624 837033
or e-mail: bookshop@enterprise.net for details.

To order please quote title, author and ISBN and your full name and address.
Cheques and postal orders should be made payable to 'Bookpost plc'.
Postage and packing is FREE within the UK
(overseas customers should add £1.00 per book).

Prices and availability are subject to change.